MW00763889

Super Sheep

Colleen Dolphin
AUTHOR

C.A. Nobens
ILLUSTRATOR

Consulting Editor, Diane Craig, M.A./Reading Specialist

ABDO
Publishing Company

Published by ABDO Publishing Company, 8000 West 78th Street, Edina, Minnesota 55439.

Printed in the United States of America, North Mankato, Minnesota
052010
092010

 PRINTED ON RECYCLED PAPER

Editor: Liz Salzmann
Content Developer: Nancy Tuminelly
Cover and Interior Design and Production: Colleen Dolphin, Mighty Media
Photo Credits: iStockphoto (catnap72), Shutterstock

Library of Congress Cataloging-in-Publication Data
Dolphin, Colleen, 1979-
  Super sheep / Colleen Dolphin.
     p. cm. -- (Farm pets)
  ISBN 978-1-61613-374-0
  1. Sheep--Juvenile literature. I. Title.
  SF375.2.D65 2011
  636.3--dc22
                        2009053100

SandCastle™ Level: Transitional

SandCastle™ books are created by a team of professional educators, reading specialists, and content developers around five essential components—phonemic awareness, phonics, vocabulary, text comprehension, and fluency—to assist young readers as they develop reading skills and strategies and increase their general knowledge. All books are written, reviewed, and leveled for guided reading, early reading intervention, and Accelerated Reader® programs for use in shared, guided, and independent reading and writing activities to support a balanced approach to literacy instruction. The SandCastle™ series has four levels that correspond to early literacy development. The levels are provided to help teachers and parents select appropriate books for young readers.

Emerging Readers
(no flags)

Beginning Readers
(1 flag)

Transitional Readers
(2 flags)

Fluent Readers
(3 flags)

SandCastle™ would like to hear from you. Please send us your comments and suggestions.
sandcastle@abdopublishing.com

Contents

Sheep

Sheep are friendly animals. They can see, smell, and hear very well. Sheep's wool can be used to make warm clothing. Sheep can be great pets!

Baby sheep are called lambs.
Shawn lets his friends pet his lamb.
She is very soft.

Sheep **graze** on grass and **clover**. They need fresh water to drink every day.

A barn protects sheep from bad weather. It keeps out animals that might harm the sheep.

Jason gives his sheep a little grain. Grain is a treat for sheep. But too much grain will make sheep sick.

Carlos holds his lamb Lenny after feeding him. Carlos takes good care of Lenny.

A Sheep Story

Jack has four soft
and **fluffy** sheep.
One sheep is very lazy
and only likes to sleep.

The other three sheep
like to jump and play.
But his lazy sheep
just sleeps all day.

Jack is worried and
doesn't know what to do.
To wake up his sheep,
he decides to yell, "Boo!"

His lazy sheep **squeals**
and jumps up off the ground.
He's done with his long nap
and starts to run around!

Did You Know?

- Sheep can hear very well.

- Sheep live for about seven years. But some can live for 20 years!

- President Woodrow Wilson kept sheep on the south lawn of the White House.

- Shaving the wool off a sheep is called *shearing*.

- Sheep can be **milked**.

Sheep Quiz

Read each sentence below. Then decide whether it is true or false!

1. Wool is used to make clothes.

2. Sheep do not **graze** on grass.

3. A barn protects sheep.

4. Too much grain makes sheep sick.

5. Ian's lazy sheep never wakes up.

Answers: 1. True 2. False 3. True 4. True 5. False

23

Glossary

clover – a small plant that has three or four leaves, and pink or white flowers.

fluffy – covered with soft hair or feathers.

graze – to eat grasses and plants.

milk – to take milk out of an animal such as a cow or sheep.

squeal – to make a loud, high-pitched cry or sound.

To see a complete list of SandCastle™ books and other nonfiction titles from ABDO Publishing Company, visit www.abdopublishing.com.

8000 West 78th Street, Edina, MN 55439 • 800-800-1312 • fax 952-831-1632